s," he thought,

s…means a little bit m

he bottom we, too, sho

dness you're not somet

they played they really PLAYED

hat is truer than true! There is no one alive who

he shape you are in! • UNLESS someone like you

r. It's not. • So, on beyond Z! It's high time you

be known. • I can't blab such blibber blubber! M

he sun is not sunny. But we can have lots of good

omorrow is another one. • You rule all the land.

e the *sky*. • I do not like green eggs and ham. I

Pop. • They only could say it just "happened to

meant what I said and I said what I meant….An

u never can tell what goes on down below! This

hings you can find if you don't stay behind! • If

u'd never been born, well then what would you

k low and think high. Oh, the THINKS you can

u try! • I learned there are troubles of more than

one kind. Some come from ahead and some

come from behind

Seuss-isms

Wise and Witty Prescriptions for Living from the Good Doctor

Random House New York

TM and © 1997 by Dr. Seuss Enterprises, L.P. All rights reserved
under International and Pan-American Copyright Conventions.
Published in the United States by Random House, Inc., New York, and
simultaneously in Canada by Random House of Canada Limited, Toronto.
http://www.randomhouse.com/seussville
ISBN: 0-679-88356-8   Library of Congress Catalog Card Number: 96-70581
Printed in Singapore   15 14 13 12 11 10 9 8 7

Introduction, by Audrey Geisel

Editor's note: *Audrey Geisel is President and CEO of Dr. Seuss Enterprises, L.P., and the widow of Theodor S. Geisel, also known by millions of readers as Dr. Seuss.*

In each book he wrote, Ted achieved not only a marvelous marriage of words and illustrations but also a truly inspired sense of nonsense.

How would he feel about a collection of his "wisdom"? I can't say for certain, but I think Ted would have been surprised as well as humbled, and then really quite pleased. After all, his books contain more sane, sensible, and just plain hilarious advice for living than most of the self-help books crowding bookstores today.

Ted often let the Cat in the Hat do the talking, as in this poem originally published in praise of Reader's Digest Condensed Books:

It has often been said
there's so much to be read,
you never can cram
all those words in your head.

So the writer who breeds
more words than he needs
is making a chore
for the reader who reads.

That's why my belief is
the briefer the brief is,
the greater the sigh
of the reader's relief is.

And that's why your books
have such power and strength.
You publish with shorth!
(Shorth is better than length.)

In shorth, I think Ted
would have approved of *Seuss-isms*.

Seuss-isms

On facing up to adversity

I learned there are troubles
Of more than one kind.
Some come from ahead
And some come from behind.

But I've bought a big bat.
I'm all ready, you see.
Now my troubles are going
To have troubles with *me!*

—*I Had Trouble in Getting to Solla Sollew*

It's a troublesome world.
All the people who're in it
are troubled with troubles
almost every minute.

Just tell yourself, Duckie,
you're really quite lucky!
Some people are much more…
oh, ever so much more…
oh, muchly much-much more
unlucky than you!

—*Did I Ever Tell You How Lucky You Are?*

Seuss-isms

On loyalty...

I meant what I said
And I said what I meant...
An elephant's faithful
One hundred per cent!
—*Horton Hatches the Egg*

...and its rewards

And the people came shouting,
"*What's all this about...?*"
They looked! And they stared
with their eyes popping out!
"My goodness! *My gracious!*"
they shouted. "MY WORD!
It's something brand new!
IT'S AN ELEPHANT-BIRD!!"

And it should be, it *should* be,
it SHOULD be like that!
Because Horton was faithful!
He sat and he sat!

—*Horton Hatches the Egg*

On equality and justice

I know, up on top
    you are seeing great sights,
But down at the bottom
    we, too, should have rights.
    —*Yertle the Turtle and Other Stories*

I'm quite happy to say
That the Sneetches got really
    quite smart on that day,
The day they decided that
    Sneetches are Sneetches
And no kind of Sneetch is the best
    on the beaches.
                    —*The Sneetches and Other Stories*

But even kings can't rule the *sky*.
                    —*Bartholomew and the Oobleck*

A person's a person, no matter how small.
                    —*Horton Hears a Who!*

And the turtles, of course…
    all the turtles are free
As turtles and, maybe,
    all creatures should be.
                    —*Yertle the Turtle and Other Stories*

Seuss-isms

On diversity

We see them come.
We see them go.
Some are fast.
And some are slow.
Some are high.
And some are low.
Not one of them
is like another.
Don't ask us why.
Go ask your mother.

—*One Fish Two Fish Red Fish Blue Fish*

On respecting your elders...

You must not
hop on Pop.

—*Hop on Pop*

...and on the times when it's okay not to

Please let me be.
Please go away.
I am NOT going
to get up today!

—*I Am NOT Going to Get Up Today!*

On activism

Plant a new Truffula. Treat it with care.
Give it clean water. And feed it fresh air.
Grow a forest. Protect it from axes
    that hack.
Then the Lorax
and all of his friends
may come back.

—*The Lorax*

UNLESS someone like you
cares a whole awful lot,
nothing is going to get better.
It's not.

—*The Lorax*

On life's mysteries

'Cause you never can tell
What goes on down below!
This pool *might* be bigger
Than you or I know!

     —McElligot's Pool

On the first Nerd

And then, just to show them,
I'll sail to Ka-Troo
And bring back an it-kutch,
A preep, and a proo,
A nerkle, a NERD,
And a seersucker, too!

     —If I Ran the Zoo

On spirituality

Then the Grinch thought of something
   he hadn't before!
"Maybe Christmas," he thought,
   "*doesn't* come from a store.
Maybe Christmas…perhaps…
   means a little bit more!"
   —*How the Grinch Stole Christmas!*

On aging

The fine-toothed comb of Time
  marches on
Through the scalp of Life.

The dull, blunt needle of Time
Sews another button on a sadly worn pair
  of underdrawers.
    —"Pentellic Bilge for Bennett Cerf's Birthday"

"I still climb Mount Everest just as
often as I used to. I play polo just as
often as I used to. But to walk down to
the hardware store I find a little bit
more difficult."
    —interview in *The New York Times Book Review*

You're in pretty good shape
for the shape you are in!
    —*You're Only Old Once!*

Seuss-isms

On being true to yourself

You have brains in your head.
You have feet in your shoes.
You can steer yourself
any direction you choose.
You're on your own.
   And you know what you know.
And *YOU* are the guy
   who'll decide where to go.
                    —*Oh, the Places You'll Go!*

Come on! Open your mouth and
   sound off at the sky!
Shout loud at the top of your voice,
   "I AM I!"
ME! I am I!
And I may not know why
But I know that I like it.
Three cheers! I AM I!
                    —*Happy Birthday to You!*

Only *you* can make your mind up!
You're the one and only one!

—*Hunches in Bunches*

Seuss-isms

On the art of eating

I do not like
green eggs
and ham!
I do not like them,
Sam-I-am.

You do not like them.
So you say.
Try them! Try them!
And you may.
Try them and you may, I say.

—Green Eggs and Ham

My uncle ordered popovers
from the restaurant's bill of fare.
And, when they were served,
    he regarded them
with a penetrating stare...
Then he spoke great Words of Wisdom
as he sat there on that chair:
"To eat these things," said my uncle,
"you must exercise great care.
You may swallow down what's solid...
BUT...you must spit out the air!"

And...as you partake of the world's
    bill of fare,
that's darned good advice to follow.
Do a lot of spitting out the hot air.
And be careful what you swallow.
                    —"My Uncle Terwilliger
            on the Art of Eating Popovers"

Seuss-isms

On success

So be sure when you step.
Step with care and great tact
and remember that Life's
a Great Balancing Act.

And will you succeed?
Yes! You will, indeed!
(98 and ¾ percent guaranteed.)
KID, YOU'LL MOVE MOUNTAINS!

—*Oh, the Places You'll Go!*

On going places

The more that you read,
the more things you will know.
The more that you learn,
the more places you'll go.
— *I Can Read with My Eyes Shut!*

Think left and think right
and think low and think high.
Oh, the THINKS you can think up
if only you try!
— *Oh, the Thinks You Can Think!*

So you see!
There's no end
To the things you might know,
Depending how far
    beyond Zebra you go!

—*On Beyond Zebra!*

SO…that's why I
tell you to keep your eyes wide. Keep them
wide open…at least on one side. • "Maybe Chri
doesn't come from a store. Maybe Christmas…pe
up on top you are seeing great sights, but down
goodness for all of the things you are not! Thank
person's a person. No matter how small. • And v
worked they really WORKED. • Today you are y
is you-er than you! • You're in pretty good shape
cares a whole awful lot, nothing is going to get l
were shown that you really *don't* know all there i
tongue isn't made of rubber. • I know it is wet a
fun that is funny! • Today is gone. Today was fu
And you rule all the people. But even kings can
do not like them, Sam-I-am. • You must not ho
happen" and was not very likely to happen agair
elephant's faithful one hundred per cent! • 'Caus
pool *might* be bigger than you or I know! • Oh,
we didn't have birthdays, you wouldn't be you.
do? • Think left and think right and
think up if onl